SISTER EDEN: Not Like the Rest of Us
by **Elfreeda Starr Miles**

ISBN: 978-1-967860-59-3

Paperback Version

Table of Contents

Chapter 1 – The News Drop......................5

Chapter 2 – Homecoming.......................8

Chapter 3 – Aunties and Theories..........13

Chapter 4 – Truck-Stop Calls................17

Chapter 5 – Uncle Theo's Visit...............20

Chapter 6 – Eden's Eyes........................24

Chapter 7 – School Years.......................29

Chapter 8 – Joyce Moves Out................34

Chapter 9 – Family Cookout...................40

Chapter 10 – Ruth Sick..........................47

Chapter 11 – The DNA Test Commercial 52

Chapter 12 – Eden's Boyfriend..............57

Chapter 13 – Ruth's Slip........................63

Chapter 14 – Uncle Theo's Mouth (Again)
....68

Chapter 15 – Ama's Logbook.................73

Chapter 16 – Joyce vs. Caleb.................81

Chapter 17 – The Test...........................87

Chapter 18 – The Blow-Up....................98

Chapter 19 – The Funeral.....................107

Chapter 20 – The Graveside Talk.........118

SISTER EDEN

Not Like the Rest of Us

Chapter 1 – The News Drop

Mama waited till the cornbread hit the table. That's how you know she knew it'd land heavy.

"Y'all," she said, folding her napkin like she was in church. "I'm pregnant."

Forks stopped mid-air. Daddy blinked once, real slow. I looked from him to Mama, back again, checking who'd laugh first. Nobody did.

"You mean... pregnant *pregnant*?" I said.

"There another kind?" she shot back.

The clock over the stove ticked like it was counting down to something. I was twenty, paying rent on a back room that used to be the laundry. My brothers were off doing what boys do—ruining cars and girls—and Mama talking about starting over.

Daddy cleared his throat. "We happy," he said. Voice flat as day-old Coke.

"Speak for yourself," I muttered, too low for Jesus but not for Mama.

She gave me that look, the one that could curdle milk. "You got a smart mouth, Joyce."

"Got it from you," I said, because if I didn't talk, I'd scream.

Next Sunday she walked into church glowing like a lightbulb that knew it shouldn't still work. The women surrounded her, all baby-talk and prophecy. Daddy smiled the way men do when they don't own the story but gotta stand in it anyway.

Nine months later, they brought her home—Eden.

"She's different," I told Mama that first night.

"She's blessed," she snapped back.

But the baby's eyes were honey-gold, not brown. Her curls were looser. And when she cried, Daddy flinched like it hurt somewhere deep.

Chapter 2 – Homecoming

The day Mama brought the baby home, rain came down in sheets like somebody upstairs had tipped a bucket. The porch sagged with the weight of cousins, aunties, and noise. Everybody wanted to see the "miracle baby," though half of them just wanted to see if what they'd heard was true.

Mama stepped out of Daddy's old Ford like she was walking into a movie. Her hair was wrapped in a scarf the color of coffee with too much cream, and her face had that new-mama glow that only lasts until the first night-feeding. Daddy followed behind her, carrying the car seat like it might explode if he tilted it wrong.

I leaned against the doorway, arms crossed. Couldn't help noticing how the baby's skin had that high-yellow tone that never showed up in our side of the family. Eyes half-open, searching. You could already tell she was going to look at people too long, like she wanted to see through them.

"Move back, Joyce, let us in," Mama said, sharp like always.

I stepped aside. The living room was too bright, every lamp on. Aunt Geraldine was already there with a camera, clicking like she'd been hired. The baby fussed, small squeaks that somehow filled the room.

Mama sat down and unwrapped the blanket. "Her name's Eden," she said. "Because she's a new beginning."

Everybody "oohed" and "aahed," like they'd never heard of sin in a garden before. I just nodded and said, "Pretty."

But something itched behind my ribs. Eden's hair was soft, fine, not tight like ours. Her nails were white and perfect.

Even her cry sounded lighter. Mama caught me staring and said, "Don't start with your comments, Joyce. God made her how He wanted."

"I didn't say nothing," I said, but she knew better.

When the crowd thinned and the last plastic cup hit the trash, I offered to do the night shift. Mama didn't argue. She went straight to bed, like relief had knocked her out cold. Daddy sat in his chair staring at the TV with the sound off. When I picked Eden up, his eyes followed me like he wanted to ask something but couldn't risk the answer.

"She hungry?" he asked.

"She just ate."

"She burp?"

"Yup."

"Good. Babies that small shouldn't cry too long. Makes 'em nervous."

"She not nervous," I said. "She just new."

He nodded, slow. "Whole house feel new."

Later, after he'd gone to bed, I fed her anyway just to keep her quiet. The bottle was warm, her fingers curling around mine, impossibly tiny. She stopped halfway through and looked up at me, eyes that weird amber color.

"You different," I whispered, same words again. "You know that?"

She blinked like she did. Rain kept tapping the window; the clock ticked too loud. I hummed something, maybe a song Mama used to sing before she stopped singing.

When I laid Eden down, I noticed her wristband still on—white plastic with letters starting to fade. "Patient: Ruth Afolayan. Time: 3:12 AM." I frowned. Mama said she went in around six. But what did I know? Maybe hospitals write things different.

I wrote it down anyway, on the back of a receipt in my pocket.

At dawn the house smelled like reheated coffee and baby wipes. Mama shuffled into the kitchen, robe hanging loose. "You didn't sleep?"

"Nah."

"She cry much?"

"Not really. Just looks around like she thinking."

Mama poured coffee, stared at the steam. "Babies don't think. They just be."

"Maybe this one do," I said.

Mama's eyes lifted to mine—flat, tired, warning. "Don't make her strange before she get a chance to be normal."

I shrugged. "Too late. She already different." That earned me silence thick enough to spread on toast.

Chapter 3 – Aunties and Theories

By the second week, folks were talking. Not loud, just enough that it floated back to me at the store, at the bus stop, and over phone lines. "Ruth done found the fountain of youth." "That baby don't look nothing like Caleb." "Maybe it skipped a generation."

Mama acted deaf. Daddy doubled his routes, hauling freight from Chicago to Memphis, staying gone longer each time. I started calling him "ghost trucker."

Eden grew fast, alert, greedy for everything. When I held her, she'd grab a handful of my hair and pull like she meant to take some with her. Sometimes Mama would just watch from the doorway, eyes glazed, like she was half-proud, half-scared.

One evening Aunt Geraldine dropped by with fried catfish and gossip. "Ruth, you sure you up for this at your age?" she said between bites. "Menopause been playing tricks lately."

Mama forced a laugh. "Guess God had other plans."

"Mm-hmm," Aunt G said, sucking her teeth. "Well, He sure mixed the recipe this time."

I choked on my sweet tea. Mama's glare could've burned paint, but Aunt G didn't notice. She reached over, touched Eden's curls. "Pretty baby though. Real pretty. Got that look like she gon' get what she want."

Mama changed the subject to laundry detergent.

After Aunt G left, I tried to lighten it. "At least she said pretty."

Mama didn't bite. "Don't entertain foolishness. People talk when they bored."

"She right though. Baby don't look like you or Daddy."

Her jaw tightened. "Go fold the clothes."

So, I did, but my mind kept running laps. I remembered how Daddy's face looked when he first saw Eden, like surprise pretending to be joy. How he flinched when she cried, then smiled too fast after. Something sat wrong, like a picture hung slightly crooked.

That night I called my friend Nina. "Girl, that baby don't match."

She laughed. "Always a conspiracy with you."

"I'm serious. You ever seen a newborn with honey eyes in a house full of black coffee?"

"Maybe the mailman fine."

"Not funny."

"Then stop talking like you on CSI. Just love the kid."

I wanted to. God knows I tried. But every time I looked at Eden, I felt this twist inside — curiosity mixed with dread, like finding a locked drawer in your own room. You don't even know what's in it yet, but you already scared to look.

Chapter 4 – Truck-Stop Calls

Daddy started running longer hauls that summer. "More miles, more money," he said, but his voice didn't match the math. He'd call from somewhere in Tennessee or Arkansas, the rumble of diesel behind him, and ask about the baby like he was checking a weather report.

"How's my girls?"

"Fine."
"She eating good?"

"She eat like she got a job." He'd chuckle, but it always sounded borrowed.

When the call ended, Mama would stand by the window, phone in her hand, staring into nothing. "He working too hard," she'd say, though we both knew she meant *he staying gone too long.*

Some nights the phone rang after midnight. His number, but not his voice right away—just highway hum, then a sigh. "Joyce, you up?"
"Yeah."
"You helping your mama?"
"Yeah."
A pause long enough to feel like truth wanted out and changed its mind. "Take care of your sister," he'd say, then hang up.

Eden started sleeping through the night around three months, which gave me more time to think—never a good thing in this house. I'd look at the pictures on the wall: me and Daddy at my high-school graduation, Mama at her sewing machine, the empty space where new baby photos should've gone but hadn't yet.

Mama hadn't taken Eden to one of those mall photo studios. Said she'd do it "when I lose this belly." But weeks passed, and the frame stayed empty.

One evening I asked, "You gonna send Daddy some pictures?" "He got eyes," she said. "He ain't here to use them." She cut her glance at me. "Mind your tone." I did, but only because the baby started crying.

Later, while folding laundry, I found a letter in the dryer vent—half-melted envelope, my father's handwriting. I smoothed it out. Just a note about gas money, a reminder to "keep receipts for taxes." No "Love you," no "miss you." Cold facts on lined paper.

I slid it back where I found it. Some things you let hide themselves.

Chapter 5 – Uncle Theo's Visit

Uncle Theo showed up three months later in a cloud of cigarette smoke and cheap cologne, carrying a six-pack and bad intentions. Daddy's brother, same eyes but heavier, mouth too quick. He hadn't been around since Grandma's funeral.

"Look at this place," he said, stepping inside like he owned rent. "Ruth still got it smelling like Pine-Sol and secrets."

Mama stiffened. "Watch your mouth around my baby."

He laughed, cracked a beer. "Which one? The old one or the new one?"

I almost choked.

Mama snatched the can from his hand. "Don't start."

"Just saying. Caleb out here driving his life away, and you—" He stopped himself, looked at me, then at Eden in her swing. "That baby sure is… bright."

"Means what?" Mama's voice dropped an octave.

Theo shrugged. "Means beautiful, sis-in-law. Don't be so touchy." He left soon after, but the air stayed thick with whatever he didn't say.

Later that night, while Mama bathed Eden, I found Theo on the porch finishing his beer. The streetlight buzzed like gossip.

"You always got something to say," I told him.

He squinted at me. "You always looking for something to hear."

"What you mean?"

He chuckled, low. "Girl, you smart. You already know what I mean."

"No, I don't."

He leaned forward, breath sour. "Ask your daddy why he been hauling loads through Memphis when the route don't pay extra. Ask him who live there."

"Who?"

Theo tapped his temple. "Some things you better learn slow. Easier on the heart." He walked off into the night, whistling off-key.

Inside, Mama was humming to the baby, water running, the house smelling like cocoa butter and warning signs. I stood there between rooms, realizing I'd never once seen Eden's hospital pictures—no bracelet, no blanket, nothing except her now.

She looked up from the tub, bubbles clinging to her chin, and smiled at me. For a second I felt stupid—like maybe suspicion was just loneliness wearing new clothes.

But then I remembered Theo's words, and the smile didn't comfort me anymore.

Chapter 6 – Eden's Eyes

By the time Eden turned five, her eyes had settled into that gold-brown that made strangers say, "What a pretty child," like pretty was a pass that excused everything else. She learned to stare people down without blinking. If you lied, she'd tilt her head and watch your mouth like she was reading subtitles.

First day of kindergarten, Mama ironed her a yellow dress that made her look like a sun you couldn't squint at long. I took pictures on my phone because Mama still hadn't been to any studio and Daddy was on a run that "might stretch to two weeks." Eden held my hand but kept pulling forward, like the school was a place she'd already decided belonged to her.

The hallway smelled like crayons and bleach. Teachers crouched to kid height, voices high and tired already. The principal, a man with a too-brown tie and a too-wide smile, said, "Welcome! You must be... Eden's grandma?"

Mama's face didn't move. "Mother," she said, syllables sharp. "I am her mother."

The principal backpedaled so hard he almost tripped on his own apology. "Of course—of course. My mistake."

Eden watched the whole exchange without saying a word, then squeezed my hand twice. On the way to her classroom she pointed at the mural of animals and named every single one like she'd painted them: "Okapi. Warthog. Shoebill." The teacher blinked like she'd been handed a spelling test by a toddler.

"Where you learn that?" I asked.

"Books," Eden said, like I was the child.

They had us stack labeled supplies. Mama set everything in neat towers: tissues, pencils, sanitizer, all bought on sale with three coupons and a prayer. A mother across the room whispered to another and looked at Mama's gray streak like it was a puzzle piece stuck in the wrong box. Eden watched that too. Her eyes got brighter when people pretended to be quiet.

"Eden," the teacher said, "what's your favorite color?"

"Not a color," she said. "Texture."

"Texture?"

"Velvet." Then she smiled like that should have been obvious, and the teacher wrote "VELVET" on a star and put it on the wall like she wasn't sure if it was a correct answer or a new kind of child she needed to prepare for.

On the walk home, Mama kept glancing at me. "You catch that?"

"Catch what?"

"The principal. The mothers. All them little looks."

"I caught it."

"Let it drop."

I nodded, but my head was still back in that room, watching Eden build an invisible boundary around herself. She was five and already a country with her own rules. You either learned the customs or you paid a fee.

That night she sat on the living room floor with a pile of library books as tall as her chest. She read out loud until the words got too hard, then made up her own version and it was better anyway. Mama hemmed a skirt at the table, needle flashing, jaw set. When Eden said, "Why your hair got silver in it, Mama?" Ruth didn't look up.

"Because time is honest," Mama said. "And honest things show."

Eden nodded like that made perfect sense and kept reading. I didn't know which part of the answer bothered me—the truth itself, or how easy my baby sister swallowed it while the rest of us choked.

Chapter 7 – School Years

Kids love difference until it gets them teased. By second grade, a girl named Maddy decided Eden's hair was "weird pretty." That turned into five girls following Eden on the playground asking if her eyes were contacts. Eden said no. They said liar. A boy pushed Eden on the shoulder to see if her balance was special too. She hit him back harder and ended up in the principal's office with a plastic chair too low for her pride.

I got the call because Mama was at the clinic with her blood pressure and Daddy was three states away pretending distance was respect. When I walked into the office, Eden was swinging her legs like she'd been born in detention. The boy had an ice pack and a surprised look, like he'd learned something important about underestimating small girls.

"What happened?" I asked Eden.

"They had questions," she said.

"You can answer without your fists."

"Depends on the question."

The principal started in with the policy talk. "Zero tolerance," "conflict resolution," "restorative conversation." Eden nodded through all of it and said "okay" in a tone that meant "hurry up."

In the car she crossed her arms. "Why they always wanna touch me?"

"Because people touch what they don't understand."

"That's nasty."

"Yep."

She stared out the window. "Joyce, you think Daddy like me?"

The question fell between the seats. I thought about all the photos he wasn't in, all the birthday dinners where he called from a parking lot. "He love you," I said.

"That's not what I asked."

I gripped the wheel. "He like you when he here."

"That's not what I asked either."

We rode the rest of the way quiet. At a light, she reached over, took my hand, squeezed it twice like on the first day of school. I squeezed back.

Third grade she started drawing maps—of the house, the block, the route to the corner store with arrows for where the dogs bark and where Mrs. Langley sometimes falls asleep on her porch. She'd tape the maps to the fridge like she was the mayor assigning permits. Mama never took them down, even when she cleaned everything else like dirt was a sin and clutter was a crime.

Fourth grade, science class did the unit on traits. Kids brought pictures; they matched dimples, earlobe shapes, tongue rolling. Eden came home with a worksheet half-done and eyes darker than usual.

"What's wrong?" I asked.

"Nothing."

"Lie better."

She slid the paper across the table. "We did eyes. Teacher said brown beats green, blue, hazel. 'Dominant.' She said if both parents got dark brown, then… then the kid probably do too."

"Probably," I said. "Not always."

She picked at the corner of the paper. "I asked if 'probably' can be wrong. She said genes roll dice. But then she looked at me like the dice were loaded."

I heard Mama in the hallway, paused like she was listening. "Folks always got charts," I said. "They don't have our story."

"What's the story?"

"Eat your chicken."

She smiled without teeth. "Bad lie, Joyce."

I swallowed. "Maybe. But you still gotta eat."

That night Mama came to my room. "Don't feed what you can't fix," she said, standing in the doorway like a ghost with rules.

"She asked."

"Then you teach her patience."

"She nine."

"Then you teach her nine kinds of patience."

I almost asked Mama for the real story. But the way she held the doorframe—like it was the only thing not moving under her feet—shut me up.

Chapter 8 – Joyce Moves Out

I moved out the summer Eden turned eleven. Not because I hated the house, but because I could smell something in it—like wires burning behind a wall—and I didn't want to be asleep when it sparked.

The apartment was a one-bedroom over a hair braiding shop. The stairs creaked like rats learning English. The windows faced brick and pigeons. I loved it like a stray loves whoever feeds it. My paycheck from the grocery store covered rent and ramen if I turned the A/C off and slept in the fridge.

I told Mama, "I'll still come by every day."

She said, "Don't make promises to soothe yourself." Then she hugged me too long and slipped forty dollars in my pocket like I was going on a school trip.

Daddy brought over a toolbox and fixed nothing. "Proud of you," he said, looking at the ceiling while he said it. "Independence is good."

"Commitment better," I said before I could catch it.

He rubbed the back of his neck. "You always been smart."

"Smart get tired."

"Yeah," he said. "It do."

Eden helped me label boxes with a thick black marker—KITCHEN, CLOTHES, BOOKS, MISC, like we were organizing grief. She drew a little map of my apartment on the back of a cereal box and taped it to my fridge. Under it she wrote: **JOYCE'S HOUSE RULES—NO**

LYING, NO THIRSTY MEN, EXTRA ORANGES ALWAYS.

"Extra oranges?" I asked.

"For when you get sad," she said. "Or sick. Or both."

"You a doctor now?"

"Not yet," she said, serious.

She slept over the first weekend. We lay on my floor and watched TV on a chair because I hadn't learned how furniture worked yet. Around midnight she said, "If you had a baby, would you tell them the truth?"

"About what?"

"Everything."

I stared at the ceiling fan, counting its slow blades. "Maybe not everything all at once."

"What about piece by piece?"

"That seems fair."

She turned on her side. "Do you think Mama like me?"

"She love you."

"That's not what I asked."

I felt the apartment shrink. "Some people show like different."

"What's Daddy's different?"

"Milk-carton different."

She laughed into the pillow, then got quiet. "I want you to be my emergency contact," she said.

"I already am."

"Not the school paper. Real life."

"Okay," I said, and we let that be a contract. She fell asleep with her hand in mine. I watched her face relax into something I wished the whole world could see before they decided who she was.

When I dropped her home Sunday, Mama had that look that means a whole page of words.

"She fine," I said.

"She always fine when she with you."

"That sound like a complaint."

"It sound like truth." Mama crossed her arms. "Don't be the fun parent if you can't be the full parent."

"I'm her sister."

"Same rules," she said, and walked away like she'd won something.

In the kitchen, the sink was full of dishes that weren't there when I picked Eden up. On the counter a stack of mail addressed to Daddy with windows for numbers Mama didn't want to see. I washed the plates, dried my hands, left a bag of oranges on the table. On my way out, Eden pressed a folded paper into my hand. "Open later," she whispered.

In the car I unfolded it at a red light. A drawing—me and her on a couch I didn't own yet, a window with sunshine I didn't have, and a caption: **WHEN WE MOVE AGAIN, MAKE SURE THERE'S ROOM FOR BOTH OF US.**

The light turned green and I drove like the world was fragile glass and me, for once, not the one dropping it.

Chapter 9 – Family Cookout

Every summer our cousins throw a cookout like they trying to feed a small army—ribs piled like firewood, card tables sagging under potato salad, dominoes smacking loud enough to register on seismographs. That year it was in Aunt G's backyard, the grass clipped to the scalp and the kids sticky with store-brand popsicles.

I showed up late with two bags of ice and a stack of dollar buns. Mama and Eden were already there. Mama wore a sundress that pretended she'd slept well all week. Eden wore the face she wore in crowds: curious, ready, on guard. Daddy texted "running behind" and never stopped running.

Cousin Tracy clocked us at the gate, lips twitching. "There go Ruth and her little twin," she said. The way she said **twin** made it sound like a dare.

Eden slipped her hand into mine without looking. "I'm gonna get lemonade."

"You want me to—"

"I can handle cups," she said, and disappeared into the cluster of coolers like a scout on a mission.

I found Aunt G near the grill, bossing the fire. "You look skinny," she said. "You eating?"

"Food costs money," I said. "I prefer breath."

She laughed, then leaned closer. "Your mama holding up?"

"Define 'up'."

"Mm. Heard Caleb ain't sleeping at home much."

"Truckers sleep on wheels."

Aunt G flipped ribs like she was turning pages. "Theo been running his mouth."

"He does cardio with it."

She cut her eyes at me. "He think he clever. He ain't. But when a man talk too much around beer, sometimes one truth slip out by mistake."

I swallowed. The smoke stung. "What truth?"

"Don't go fishing in my yard," she said, then softened. "Eat something. You hold anger and low blood sugar at the same time, you gon' end up in jail."

By the card table Uncle Theo was already three drinks in, telling a story nobody asked for. Eden set her lemonade down and stood where she could hear without being seen. He noticed her anyway—Theo always noticed the exact person who shouldn't hear him.

"Look at that one," he said, nodding toward Eden like she was the weather. "Pretty as a sin on payday."

"Shut up, Theo," Aunt G snapped from the grill.

"I'm complimenting! Can't compliment family no more?" He smirked, then leaned back. "Caleb lucky. Some men got to go searching for excitement. Some men get it delivered."

The table laughed too loud, the way people laugh when they don't know the rules anymore. Eden's mouth thinned. She picked up her cup and walked away.

I caught up by the fence. "You okay?"

She didn't answer. She stared at the crooked plank where somebody carved initials years back. "People talk like I'm furniture," she said.

"They talk like they ain't met themselves yet."

She looked at me. "Why you always sound like a fortune cookie when you don't want to tell the truth?"

I took a breath. The music thumped; a child cried; somebody yelled "spades!" like a battle cry. "Because I don't have the truth you're asking for."

"Then get it," she said, and walked toward the kiddie pool where little cousins were making soup out of grass and water.

Later, as the sun sagged and mosquitoes held a convention, Daddy finally appeared, smelling like diesel and mint gum. He hugged Mama quick, patted Eden's head like she was a dog that might bite. When he saw Theo, his jaw set.

"You been drinking," Daddy said.

"You been disappearing," Theo answered.

"Leave."

Theo stood up, swayed. "You gon' make me?"

Daddy didn't move. He didn't have to. Aunt G pointed the basting brush at Theo like a wand. "Get out my yard before I baptize you in hot grease."

Theo held his hands up and smiled that crooked smile. "All right, saints. I'm going." He pointed at me as he passed. "You always wanted answers, Joyce. Careful what you wish for. They heavy when you carry 'em."

He left to a chorus of side-eyes. Daddy watched him go, then turned to me like I'd been the one talking. "Don't let him get in your head."

"He already living there," I said. "Pays rent late, too."

Daddy looked at Eden across the yard, talking to a little cousin, making a crown out of dandelions and stubbornness. He rubbed his temple and said, so soft I almost missed it, "I tried."

"Tried what?"

But he'd already stepped away, toward the ribs and the men, where words were easier.

That night, in my apartment, I sat on the edge of my bed and replayed every glance, every half sentence, every almost. The city quieted down to its bones. My phone buzzed—Eden, a photo: her dandelion crown tilted, her smile all teeth and defiance. Caption: **QUEEN OF NOTHING. FOR NOW.**

I wrote back: **Queen of Not Lying. Always.**

Three dots bubbled, stopped, bubbled again. Then: **Then why won't you?**

I put the phone face down and stared at the ceiling till it blurred. Outside, somewhere, a siren started. Inside, something else did.

Chapter 10 – Ruth Sick

The cough started in January, the kind that sounds like a drawer getting slammed shut. Mama said it was "a winter tickle," then "just my sinuses," then "leave me alone, Joyce." By the time she admitted it was anything, she was two weeks into wheezing and trying to hide the wheezing like it was a bill she could stuff behind the microwave.

I took her to the urgent care on 4th. Everything in there was beige and humming. The nurse put a cuff on her arm and frowned when it squeezed. "Blood pressure's skating high," she said, cheerful like a bad news welcome mat. Mama put her mouth in that thin line that means "don't say my business out loud." We left with two prescriptions, both of which she said made her feel worse. She cut the pills in half because "half the price and half the side effects," like medicine worked like coupons.

I started stopping by her house before work and after—checking her chest, hearing that paper-bag crinkle in her breath. Eden acted casual, which with her means extra helpful. "I can do laundry," she said. "I can cook." Then burned rice and laughed, then tried again until the pot surrendered and became food.

In the quiet corners, the house started telling on us. The stack of mail with Daddy's name and a Memphis return address from a parts distributor he didn't deliver for. A photo magnet on the fridge with a chip in the corner—used to be all of us at the county fair; now the chip had knocked Daddy's face into a blur, and nobody'd replaced it. In the hallway closet: a shoebox of receipts rubber-banded too tight, and on top, a loose Polaroid of Mama at a picnic table with a man I didn't know, the picture so overexposed it looked like a ghost had leaned in and smudged him out.

I slid it back like I hadn't seen it.

One night after the clinic, Mama sat on the edge of her bed and pressed the heel of her hand to her sternum. "Hurts where the truth sits," she said, half-joke, half-prayer.

"Drink some water," I told her. "I'll make tea."

"You think tea fixes everything."

"It fixes the part of me that need to do something."

She looked at me long. "You got that from me."

"Which part?"

"The part that can't leave a knot untied."

"I'm not untying anything," I said. "Just keeping you breathing."

"Same thing."

She lay down and turned her face to the wall. In the doorway I watched her shoulders quiver under the blanket, the cough catching and missing, catching and missing like a jump rope nobody could keep rhythm with anymore. I wanted to crawl under the covers myself and be twelve again, ask her to promise me things she couldn't promise, hold me like answers were warm.

Instead, I washed a mug and set a pill by it and texted Eden to pick up ginger on her way home. "Get the ugly kind," I wrote. "The ugly ones work better."

Eden texted back a selfie with her tongue out and the ginger in a bag. Caption: **Got the ugliest. For the strongest tea.**

I showed Mama the picture. She smiled around the edges. "That girl," she said, which is how Mama said *light of my life* without using the words.

"Yeah," I said. "That girl."

Then—because the room was too full of old air—I went to the sink and ran the tap and let the sound pretend to be rain.

Chapter 11 – The DNA Test Commercial

Eden and I were on my couch on a Saturday, half-watching some true crime show where the husband never did it until he absolutely did it, when a commercial came on for one of those spit-in-a-tube ancestry kits. You know the ones—white background, happy music, a lady twirling around with two different flags because she found out she's 4% something she can use for a recipe.

Eden laughed through her nose. "Look at them. Finding out their cousins with soup."

"Soup slaps," I said. "Don't disrespect soup."

She leaned forward, elbows on knees. The ad did that thing where they show faces dissolving into maps—somebody's cheekbone becoming a coastline. Eden's mouth tilted. "You ever want to know that bad?" she asked. "Where you made of?"

"Sometimes," I said. "Then I remember I got rent."

She didn't laugh. The commercial ended in a swirl of family trees. Eden was still staring at the blank TV like it had more to say. "If I did it," she asked, "you think Mama would be mad?"

"About spit in a tube?"

"About what spit might tell."

I reached for the remote, found nothing useful to click. "Depends on what it says."

"Depends on what *she* says," Eden corrected.

"Also that."

She turned to me. Her hair was wrapped up in a scarf patterned like a topographical map; sometimes she did that on purpose—match the shapes of the day. "Joyce," she said. "If you knew a thing that would hurt me but help me breathe, would you tell me?"

I felt the floor tilt under us. "What if the telling is the hurting."

"What if the not-telling is too." She didn't say it mean. Just factual, like weather.

"Most things are both," I said.

She groaned, flopped back on the couch. "You love an answer that don't answer."

"I'm my mother's daughter."

She threw a pillow at me. "That's the question, though, ain't it?"

We let the room cool around us. Outside, a siren ran past and didn't stop. On the coffee table Eden's maps overlapped—

my block, Mama's block, the route to the clinic, the shortcut to the good empanadas from Mr. Rivera's cart. She tapped the one that led to home.

"I want to know what road I came on," she said, almost whispering. "All of it. Even if it's full of potholes."

"Then ask," I said.

"I did."

"Ask again."

"Who?"

"You know who."

She closed her eyes. "She'll say *hush*."

"Then say *no*."

She opened one eye and looked at me. "You gonna stand behind me when I do?"

"Behind you," I said. "Beside you. In front of you if I have to take something first."

She sat up and hugged me rough, the way she always hugged when words made her itchy. On the TV, the next show started—somebody else's secrets lined up for us like a buffet. We ate the popcorn anyway.

Chapter 12 – Eden's Boyfriend

He showed up with a toolbox and a grin—name was Malik, but he said everybody called him Lake 'cause he soaked up more than he should and reflected whatever stood too close. He had a mechanic's hands and a barber's edge-up and a laugh you could hear from the sidewalk.

Eden told me not to be a hater. "He's kind," she said.

"Kind gets heavy if it ain't got a job," I said.

"He got two."

"Good. Let one of them be patience."

They met at the tire shop where he mounted new rubber on her beat-up Corolla and refused to charge her for air. She said he didn't try any lines; he asked what book she was reading and actually listened. He carried her maps like they were art. He had that exact mixture of charm and honesty that make girls forgive late texts and missing toothbrushes.

He came over for dinner the second week. Brought peach soda and a bag of chips like a teenager and set them on my counter with prayers in his eyes. "I can cook," he said. "I make a mean omelet."

"We eating rice and stew," I told him.

"I can chop."

"Chop," I said. He chopped. He hummed while he chopped, something without words, the kind of tune men make when they're happy with their hands.

Mama liked him immediately, which made me suspicious. She gave him the "you better treat my baby right" speech but with a smile, and he nodded like an altar boy. After dinner he offered to fix the loose cabinet door. While he was under the sink he said, casual, "Ms. Ruth, you from around here?"

"Been around here," Mama said.

"Mr. Caleb too?"

"Off and on."

"You two make a bright kid," he said, still halfway under the sink. "No disrespect. I'm just saying—Eden got a look that ain't common."

Mama's mouth did that click. "What kind of look?"

He slid out, wiped his hands. "Like somebody turned the saturation up on her. Like the rest of y'all sepia and she Kodak."

I knew he meant it as a compliment. It sounded like a verdict.

After he left, Eden glowed like a new penny. "He's real," she said. "He don't pretend."

"I see that," I said.

"You don't like him."

"I didn't say that."

"   You didn't have to."

I sighed. "I like that he sees you. That's rare."

"And—"

"And I don't like that he sees the questions, too."

"You think I don't see them?"

"I think you live inside them."

She nodded slow. "Good. Then we can stop pretending they not the walls."

Two nights later we were all at Mama's again because the cough had gotten worse and the cheap inhaler made her jitter. Eden sat by her bed, rubbing

Vicks on her chest like an old wives' tale that still works. Lake leaned in the doorway, hands in pockets, respectful.

"You want tea?" he asked Mama.

"I want quiet," she snapped, then softer, "Sorry. Yes. Tea."

He went to the kitchen like he lived there. I watched him with a small hunger I didn't expect—jealous, maybe, of how easily some men make themselves useful.

As he passed me, he whispered, "Joyce, can I ask you something without you cussing me out?"

"Unlikely," I said. "Try."

He glanced back toward the bedroom. "You sure y'all blood?"

There it was. Like a beer bottle rolling under a seat—you knew it was there; didn't know when it would clink. I kept my face forward. "You sure you my business?"

He held up both hands. "My bad. I just—look, I grew up in a house full of steps and half's and God-know-what. People turned mean 'cause adults couldn't say what happened and kids had to smell it anyway. I'm just trying to make sure nobody sink when the boat start rocking."

"The boat already rocking," I said.

He nodded. "Then get life jackets."

I didn't answer. He made the tea. We took it to Mama. She said thank you without looking at him, and he stood in the doorway like a man measuring whether he belonged.

On his way out he tapped the map on the fridge—Eden's latest, a hurricane of arrows. "She draw like she trying to save us," he said.

"Maybe she is."

He looked at me, serious. "Then save her back."

Chapter 13 – Ruth's Slip

Fever hit on a Thursday. One of those sweats that soaks the sheets and leaves your hair stuck to your temples like you've been running from something that can run faster. Mama tried to sit up; her head said no. The clinic had one doctor on duty and five people ahead coughing into the same air. I took her home instead and did the old-fashioned things—cold cloth, Tylenol, soup with too much garlic.

Eden came straight from work in scrubs, all gentle hands and bossy voice. "Drink," she said, and Mama drank because babies in scrubs make even stubborn people behave.

It wasn't until three in the morning that Mama started talking to the ceiling. Fever talk is a language I hate—it opens doors you can't close back right. She mumbled first: "not today, not like that, not my house." Then clearer: "I told him no," and "Caleb, you said okay," and then she said a name I didn't know and then said, "that man's child," and for a second the air in the room left.

Eden froze. The washcloth hung over the bowl, drip, drip. "What she say?" she asked, voice thin.

"Fever dreams." My mouth did the lie. My heart did the truth.

"Joyce," Eden said, like a warning and a prayer.

Mama kept going. "God forgive me, God forgive me," then something about Memphis, then "don't tell, don't tell."

Eden stood up so fast the chair skittered. "Fuck this," she said, quiet and final, and left the room. Not a teenager stomp; a grown woman exit.

I followed her to the kitchen. She had her hands pressed to the counter like she was trying to stop it from moving. Her face was dry; her eyes were not. "I'm done," she said.

"You're tired," I said.

"I'm done with tired. I want true." She looked at me, and there wasn't a lick of begging in it, only demand. "What happened."

"I don't—"

"Don't," she said. "If you say you don't know, I'm gonna leave and I might not come back."

The fridge hummed like it was nervous. I sat. My knees shook. "I know pieces," I said. "Not the whole picture."

"Give me the corners," she said. "I'll fill the middle."

I told her about Theo's first slip, about the Memphis routes that didn't pay right, about the Polaroid with a ghost-man blur, about the mail with the parts company address, about the questions nobody let be questions. I did not say the part where I saw Mama kiss a man by the farmer's market when I was nineteen—I don't know why I kept that one like a coin under my tongue. Maybe because it hurt in a way that made me feel twelve again and I didn't want that feeling in the room.

Eden listened without blinking. When I stopped, she nodded like she was writing on her own secret paper. "I'm ordering a test," she said.

"Spit in a tube?"

"Blood. The kind that goes to chain of custody and comes back with nobody able to argue."

"Daddy..."

She flinched. "Say father."

"Father," I said. It tasted strange.

"I'm not trying to ruin him," she said. "I'm trying not to drown."

In the bedroom, Mama moaned a name again—maybe the same one; maybe the fever inventing. I wanted to put my hands over her mouth and hold the words in until the morning took them back. Instead, I went to the sink and ran water and let the sound be the thing we stared at until we could breathe.

Chapter 14 – Uncle Theo's Mouth (Again)

I didn't have to go looking for Theo; he found me, like a headache. He knocked on my apartment door two nights later, half-drunk on a Tuesday in a shirt that used to fit. "You home?" he yelled, as if the hallway needed to know my business to feel fulfilled.

I cracked the door but didn't let him in. He peered around me like I was scenery. "You ain't got no man here?" he asked, then laughed at his own joke.

"What do you want."

He leaned on the frame. "Saw your mama at the clinic. You girls got her looking like a ghost snuck up and wore her to the store."

"That sentence make sense to you?" I asked.

He squinted like I'd used algebra. "I'm checking on family."

"You don't check on people; you watch them fall."

He made a hurt face he didn't earn. "You always been mean."

"Say what you came to say, Theo. Then get."

He looked down the hall, then back at me, then lowered his voice for the first time in his life. "You know," he said. "About the girl."

"Use her name."

"Eden," he corrected, too soft. "You know Caleb ain't—"

"Yes."

He nodded like a man relieved to finally be caught. "Caleb knew too. Didn't want to. Did anyway."

My throat tightened. "Why Memphis," I asked. "What the hell in Memphis."

Theo picked at a cuticle like the truth was stuck there. "A warehouse rep. Parts guy. Tall, light eyes. Met your mama when Caleb got laid over, back when they was arguing about money and mortgages and who forgets trash night. Man name Leon, or Lionel—something that bragged about itself when you said it. That was a long time ago. Caleb found out later. Decided to… you know—"

"Raise the baby," I said.

"Love the woman," he said.

We stood there like idiots in a doorway with the world rearranging itself around our ankles. "Why didn't you say something when it mattered," I asked. "Before it made a mess out of all of us."

He smirked, a tired smirk. "When does it matter, Joyce? Before a thing breaks or after? Seems like with y'all, it always breaks during."

I wanted to punch him in the chest. I wanted to hug him because he looked like a broken boy under the beer. I settled for closing the door a little in his face and letting him keep talking to the wood.

Through it he said, "Your daddy loved you enough to lie. Your mama loved herself enough to let him. That's all the math, baby girl."

"Don't call me that," I said, and shut him out.

I leaned on the door until the hallway went silent. Inside my apartment, the quiet sounded like someone had cut the wires to the world. I sat on the floor and breathed shallow until shallow became full enough to stand up on.

I texted Eden one sentence: **His name might be Leon. Memphis. Parts company.** She wrote back immediately: **Got it.**

Then: **You okay?**

I wrote: **No. But I'm standing.**

She sent a heart. No emoji ever looked less cute.

Chapter 15 – Ama's Logbook

Miss Ama lives three houses down from Mama and knows more than Google but charges cheaper. She's been everybody's babysitter since '89 and keeps her life in a little stack of black-and-white composition books, the kind with the marbled cover and a strip of duct tape on the spine. She logs everything—pickups, drop-offs, who brought diapers, who forgot, who paid on time, who "will catch me Friday, baby." When we were kids, she wrote **JOYCE—AFTER SCHOOL** in neat block letters and next to it little notes like **SAD TODAY** or **ATE ALL THE PIZZA THEN SAID SHE DIDN'T** like she was keeping evidence for and against us.

Eden went to see her because Eden believes in paper. I went along because I believe in witnesses. We brought Miss Ama a box of donut holes and a bottle of that smell-good hand lotion from the beauty supply that claims it's made with money and miracles.

She let us in like we were overdue and made us sit at her kitchen table, which has heard more secrets than any therapist's couch. "What you want to know," she said without preamble, "and why you want to know it now."

Eden didn't do the pre-lie dance. "I want the day I came home," she said. "What you remember that ain't what I been told."

Ama's mouth tugged. "I remember your eyes," she said. "Like a lamp left on in the daytime. I remember your sister saying 'different' and your mama saying 'hush.'"

Eden smiled without smiling. "And the hours?"

Ama stood, went to the cabinet above the fridge, pulled down the stack of notebooks and a plastic sandwich bag full of old Polaroids and receipts. She flipped to the one marked **JULY–AUGUST, 20** and smoothed the page with her palm.

"Here," she said, tapping. The handwriting was tiny and decisive.

July 18, 6:10 AM – Ruth called. Said, 'On our way.' 8:35 AM – Caleb dropped off the boys. Said leaving town by 10. 3:12 AM – [previous page] Hospital called? No—Ruth texted? Time wrong? Note says 'bracelet says 3:12.'

I stared. "You wrote that?"

She nodded. "Joyce told me to remember. Said it felt important."

"I did?"

"You always been a librarian without a building."

Eden traced the 3:12 with her finger like it might smear. "What else."

Ama turned the page. **July 19, 4:40 PM – Baby in house. Name not said. Ruth quiet. Caleb quiet. Joyce loud in her eyes. 5:05 PM – Man dropped off bag— formula, diapers. Not Caleb. Said, 'Tell Ruth I kept my word.' Didn't come in. Light-skinned. Scar on jaw.**

The room leaned to one side. "You wrote that and didn't—" I started, then stopped, because Ama tilted her head at me in that way that means *be careful with your mouth in my kitchen.*

"Who was he?" Eden asked, voice flat.

"I did not ask names in that season," Ama said. "Names make you responsible."

"You wrote the scar."

"I wrote what I saw."

"Why didn't you tell—"

"Tell who, baby?" Ama's eyebrows went stern. "Your mama who already

76

decided? Your daddy who was trying to swallow a stone? You, who was sleeping in a bassinet like a secret with a bow?"

Silence did that heavy sit. Eden flipped the notebook slowly until the duct tape crackled. In the bag of old photos, Ama found a Polaroid of a table with a grocery sack on it—the same grocer we still go to, same brand of formula. And next to the sack a receipt with a name scrawled where the cashier would have written the customer's if they asked for it printed: **Leon.** No last name. No address. Just ink that looked like it had somewhere to be.

Eden looked like someone had given her a glass of water that was half gasoline. She wanted to drink. She wanted to light a match. "Can I take a picture," she asked, and Ama nodded. Eden snapped the page, the photo, the receipt. She stared at the picture on her screen like proof can heal. It can't, but it can hold your hand while you break.

"You done?" Ama asked gently.

Eden swallowed. "No. But I can't do more today."

Ama closed the book and patted it like a sleeping cat. "Truth ain't medicine," she said. "It's surgery. You still gotta heal after."

On the porch, the afternoon was the kind of hot that makes even lies sweat. Eden stopped at the top step and sat. Her hands were steady, which scared me more than if she'd shaken.

"You mad at me?" I asked. "For not making it faster?"

She shook her head. "I'm mad at the general idea," she said. "Not at you."

"You gonna tell her?" I meant Mama.

She nodded once. "Yeah. But not for permission."

"And him?" I meant Daddy. Father. The man who carried my science projects and then disappeared into mileage.

Eden's mouth trembled for the first time all day. "He already knew, didn't he."

I nodded because lying would burn the whole house down. "I think so."

She let out something between a laugh and a sob. "Then we all been actors in a play without a script."

"We had a script," I said. "It just wasn't ours."

She stood, squared her shoulders, and looked down the block toward home. "Okay," she said, and it wasn't okay but it was the best word available. "Okay."

We walked back carrying nothing but air and a phone full of dangerous pictures. Somewhere between Ama's porch and Mama's front door, I felt something leave us. Maybe it was the last bit of pretending. Maybe it was the kind of faith that keeps kids from asking better questions. A breeze picked up and flipped the hem of Eden's shirt. She held it down with one hand and with the other reached for mine and squeezed twice—the old code, the first day of school, the promise.

I squeezed back. She didn't let go.

Chapter 16 – Joyce vs. Caleb

I catch Daddy at a truck stop off I-55 that smells like diesel and cinnamon rolls that never met butter. He's leaning on the hood of the Freightliner like it's the only thing that knows his secrets. Sun's low, sky the color of an old bruise. He looks smaller next to all that machine.

"Joyce," he says, like maybe he ordered me and forgot.

"We need to talk."

He nods toward the diner. Inside, the coffee is violent and the waitress calls everybody "baby" like that's a spell. He orders eggs and doesn't touch them. I order nothing and touch everything—napkin, fork, my own fingers.

"You knew," I say.

He rubs his temple, then his chest like there's a button there that turns the day off. "About what."

"Don't start."

He exhales. "I knew."

"How long."

"Before she was born. After. Every day after that."

The coffee between us goes cold enough to see itself. "And you let me— you let *us*—walk around inside a lie."

"I walked with you," he says, soft. "That counts."

"Counts for what."

"For love," he says. "For choosing a house instead of a crater."

I want to throw the sugar packets at him. I want to hug him until one of us stops breathing. "Who is he," I ask. "Memphis. Leon."

His eyes flicker at the name. He doesn't ask how I know. "Man from a parts place," he says. "Met your mama when my truck broke down and my mouth was full of pride and our bank account was full of not enough. He talked nice. I talked mean. That's the first math."

"Did you… want to kill him?"

He laughs without humor. "I wanted to kill time. I thought if I drove enough miles the truth couldn't catch me."

"It caught us," I say.

He nods. "Truth always got better shoes."

A busboy drops a tray. Everybody jumps but me. I'm already in that dropped place. "Why didn't you leave," I ask. "Why didn't you stay and tell."

He looks at his hands. Grease lives in the lines like it pays rent. "Leaving is easy. Staying is slow heroics. I ain't no hero, Joyce. I was a man who picked a pain I knew how to carry."

"What about *her.*" I don't say Eden's name because it might break something if I do. "She been swallowing this house and no one gave her water."

He closes his eyes. "I tried to love that girl so steady she'd never notice the gap."

"She noticed the shape of it," I say. "She smart like that."

He opens his eyes and there's a wet at the corners he tries to blink back. "What she want to do."

"She's doing a test."

He flinches like I slapped him. "Chain of custody?"

"Yeah."

"You going with her."

"Yeah."

He nods. "Okay."

"Okay, what."

"Okay, I'll go too."

"You don't have to." My voice comes out sharper than I mean. "It's not… it's not about you proving a thing. It's about her not drowning in guesses."

He reaches for my hand, stops, pulls back like touching me requires a license he doesn't have. "I know," he says. "But if she's going to hear an ugly sentence, I want to be sitting in the same room when it lands."

We sit there with the eggs getting cold and the coffee mean and the waitress calling someone else "baby" two booths over. Outside, trucks glide in and out like whales surfacing.

"You ever going to tell me the whole story," I ask.

He tilts his head. "You think there is one."

"There always is."

He looks out the window at the sky that can't decide if it's done for the day. "Another time," he says, which is our family's way of saying *there was never a time that didn't hurt and I never learned how to pick one.*

When we stand, he looks older than he did when we sat. "Tell Eden I'll be there," he says.

"You tell her," I say. "Be the kind of man who uses his own mouth."

He nods like I've given him a hard job and a map. He squeezes my shoulder in that careful way like I might break from both directions.

I drive home with the window cracked, let air whip my face until I feel a little less like a glass that got bumped off a counter and knows it.

Chapter 17 – The Test

The clinic sits in a strip mall between a tax place that opens only from January to April and a vape shop that's always open. The waiting room is tired. The magazines are four summers ago. A TV on the wall plays a loop of people smiling down at paperwork like it's not going to ask for their mother's maiden name and their blood type and their ability to forgive.

Eden wears black like it's a uniform. Lake sits on one side of her, bouncing his foot, good at silence when it counts. I'm on the other side holding a clipboard that holds me back from screaming. Five chairs down, a man in a suit looks like he came to confirm something that will cost him.

Caleb walks in on time. He looks like he's been driving all night and praying the whole way. He nods at me, at Eden, at Lake. He doesn't try to hug. Eden doesn't stand. They look at each other in that way people do when love was a road and then somebody moved the street signs.

"Eden Afolayan?" the receptionist chirps.

We follow her past a poster about paternity testing that looks like it's trying not to look sad. The phlebotomist is kind and brisk. "Chain of custody means I check your IDs, watch the whole collection," she says. "Sign here, here, here." We sign like we're getting married. We sign like we're getting divorced.

They swab cheeks, fill vials. Caleb stares at the ceiling while the needle goes into his arm, like there's a generous explanation up there if he keeps looking. Eden doesn't flinch. She stares right at me, then right at the label on her own tube like she wants to memorize the bar code and the font.

"How long," she asks.

"Results in five to seven business days," the phlebotomist says. "We'll call you for pickup. No email."

"Good," Eden says, as if an email could kill her.

On the way out, we pass another room where a mom is trying to keep a toddler from climbing a chair. The kid looks at Eden like she might be a new toy. Eden sticks her tongue out once, quick, makes the kid laugh. Then we are outside and the air is too bright for the day we just had.

At the curb, nobody wants to be the one to say *I love you* and nobody wants to be the one to say *I'm sorry* in case the words stick wrong.

Caleb clears his throat. "Thank you," he tells Eden.

"For what," she says, not mean, just empty.

"For letting me show up," he says. "Some doors stay closed."

She nods like she'll file that sentence somewhere out of direct sunlight. "Okay."

He looks at Lake the way men look at other men when they have questions only a fist can ask. "You treating her right," he says.

Lake nods. "Trying. Every day."

"Trying is what her whole life been about," Caleb says. "Make it doing."

Lake says, "Yes, sir," without the sir sounding like surrender.

We split to cars like survivors leaving a crash site. In my rearview I watch Caleb stand there with his hands in his jacket, looking like a man who finally found an address and is realizing it isn't a house, it's a set of coordinates for a storm.

The days after are slow and jangly. Eden goes to work and comes back and sits at my table tracing the same line on the same map with the same pencil until the lead is a stub. "It'll say what it says," she repeats like a liturgy. "And then I'll say what I say."

Mama is quieter than quiet. I don't tell her the date. She knows anyway. She can hear when shoes are taken off at the doors of hard rooms. She watches TV with the sound low and the captions on like the house is hard of hearing.

On the fifth business day the clinic calls. "Ready for pickup."

Eden and I drive over in a silence that feels practical. Lake wants to come; Eden tells him no and kisses his forehead like a thank-you note. She signs at the window. A clerk hands over a white envelope with her name typed clean in the middle. I want to set it on fire and warm my hands and be done. She tucks it into her backpack like a bomb with a timer.

"Home," she says.

"At Mama's," I say.

"At Mama's," she agrees.

When we walk in, the house freezes like it heard shots and doesn't know where to duck. Mama at the table. Caleb on the couch. Both of them stand, then think better of it.

"We got it," Eden says, and her voice is one line on a page that doesn't break.

"Open here?" Caleb asks.

"Where else," Eden says. "Tired of other rooms owning our facts."

I sit. Lake isn't here but his mint gum is in my pocket and I chew it like it can keep me from saying something I'll regret. Eden opens the bag, then the envelope, then the inner envelope with the little black tabs you have to split with a fingernail. Paper on paper. A seal broken.

She reads. Twice. The letter makes its own weather in her face: wind then lightning then aftermath.

"What it say," Mama asks, even though she knows, even though she asks like the words might change if they come out of someone else's mouth.

"Exclusion," Eden says, crisp and quiet. "Zero percent probability Caleb is the biological father."

Caleb inhales like he forgot how. "Okay," he says. "Okay." He says it like a man trying to locate the floor.

Mama sits. She puts her hand on the table like she could stop it from trembling if the table would act right. "Eden," she says. "Baby."

"Don't 'baby' me," Eden says. "Use my name. You named me after a place we got kicked out of for eating the wrong thing."

Caleb looks at me like I might help. I can't. My mouth is a welded-shut box.

Mama clears her throat, finds the voice she uses when the receipt doesn't match the sale. "We can talk," she says. "We should talk."

"Talk is how we got here," Eden says. "Talk without truth."

"Then here it is," Mama says. "I made a mistake."

Eden laughs, a dry thing. "Mistake is when you grab nutmeg instead of cinnamon. Mistake is when you forget the rent grace period. What you made was a *decision.*"

Caleb steps forward. "It was ours," he says. "Mine too."

Eden looks at him like he's offered her a pebble while she drowns. "You can't absorb it for me," she says. "You can't swallow it and make me clean."

"I can try," he says.

"I don't want your try right now," she says. "I want her honesty."

The room turns to Ruth. For a second I see her as two people—the girl who made a choice and the woman who's been carrying it like broken glass in her pocket.

She straightens. "I was lonely and stupid and angry and wanted to hurt your father for not being what I wanted when I wanted it. A man said pretty things in my worst week and I believed them on purpose. I didn't think about later. Then later came." She breathes. "And I looked at you and I saw light and I said to hell with the rest of it."

Eden flinches at *light*. "Don't make me your redemption arc," she says. "I'm a person, not your sermon."

Mama nods once. "You're a person. And I lied to you to keep my life from collapsing. I'm not asking you to like it. I'm telling you what I did."

"And him?" Eden asks. "Leon."

Mama swallows. "He's alive. I checked last year." Her eyes flash to Caleb, then down. "He wanted to see you when you were small. I said no. I was scared he'd take you or not take you and both sounded like losing. So I made a rule and pretended it was wisdom."

Eden's chair scrapes back. The sound is a blade. "Say his last name."

"Barker," Mama says, and the word sits between us like a stray dog that might bite.

Eden nods, like something inside her mainlined electricity. "Okay."

Caleb reaches for her shoulder. She steps away. "Don't," she says, not cruel, just done. She picks up the envelope, tucks it back into the bag, and then she's moving, door, porch, air.

"Eden," Mama says, standing too fast, knocking her knee on the table hard enough to cry out.

Eden doesn't turn. She walks to the curb where the map of our block lives in her bones. Lake pulls up like he could feel the quake from his place. She gets in. He looks at me once, and I tilt my head—go. He goes.

In the doorway, Caleb leans his head against the frame the way I've seen him lean it against church doors and the backs of trucks and my graduation hall. "Ruth," he says. It's not a question. It's not an answer.

Mama sits back down. Her hands are flat on the table, palms down, like she's holding a paper from blowing away. Tears come, but quiet, like she doesn't trust them, like they might tell on her, too.

I pick up the fallen chair and set it right. Nobody sits in it.

Chapter 18 – The Blow-Up

The fight finds us two days later because of course it does. Eden comes back to the house with her backpack zipped all the way up and the kind of calm that means a storm is taking notes.

"I want the box," she says.

"What box," Mama asks, too smooth.

"The one in the hall closet with the rubber bands that cut your fingers when you pull them. The one with the receipts and the Polaroid with the ghost man who is not a ghost. The one where you keep the parts of the truth you were hoping the moths would eat."

Mama stares at the TV like it might show a show where this conversation goes better. "You don't need that."

"Want," Eden says. "I *want* that."

Caleb stands. "Let me," he says.

"No," Eden says, sharp. "You're not the vault. You're the guard who fell asleep."

He sits like she pushed him with two fingers.

Mama doesn't move. Eden walks past us down the hall, opens the closet, climbs the stepstool, and drags the box down. Rubber bands snap like little whips. Paper spills. The Polaroid skids under the coffee table. I pick it up: Mama younger, the table, the bag, the edge of a jawline that belongs to a man who eats other people's certainty.

Eden spreads the papers like she's dealing cards for a game nobody wanted to play: grocery slips, cash transfers, a hospital visitor badge that says **L. BARKER** in the ink of a bored volunteer, a thank-you note in a handwriting I don't recognize that says **Bless you** with too many loops.

"Do you want me to hurt," Eden asks, voice very even. "Or do you just not care if I do."

Mama's face cracks. "I never wanted you to hurt."

"You did it anyway."

"I wanted to protect you."

"From what," Eden says. "Reality?"

"From *men*," Mama says, and the word comes out tasting like metal. "From being a line on somebody's list. From being taken and dropped. From me."

Eden stops moving. The papers fluttering from her hand go quiet. "From you."

"Yes," Mama says. "From me. Because I was a person before I was your mother and I did a person's thing, and I didn't trust myself to handle you like a mother should." Her voice shreds. "I thought if I kept you inside the lie, you'd be safe."

Eden laughs, wild and thin. "Safe like a glass inside a house on fire."

"We put it out," Caleb says, and we both look at him like he said the wrong answer on purpose. He holds up his hands. "We tried," he corrects.

"You tried to make it pretty," Eden says. "I would've settled for true."

The volume goes up fast. Old arguments sneak in wearing new clothes. Dishes on the counter become props. A mug throws itself off the edge. The porch light catches a stray elbow later and dies with a pop like a short story.

Lake shows up without knocking. "Hey," he says, palms out. "Hey."

Eden stands with her backpack on like she's already half out the door and half twelve years old. "I'm leaving," she says. "For a while. I'll send an address."

"You can't just—" Mama starts.

"I can," Eden says. "You did."

Caleb takes a step toward her and stops again, learning the distance all over. "I love you," he says. It sounds like a confession and a theft at the same time.

She closes her eyes. "I know," she says. "It doesn't fix geometry."

"What."

"The angles," she says, opening her eyes. "The way this house sits in my head."

She turns to Mama. "Say you're sorry."

"I am," Mama says, fast.

"For the lie," Eden says. "Not for the baby I was."

Mama breathes. "I am not sorry for you," she says, careful. "I am sorry for what I made you carry."

"Okay," Eden says, and something in her shoulders loosens, then tightens back—relief and rage holding hands.

"Where you going," I ask.

"Another couch," she says, shrugging. "Another quiet. A hotel for a week if I can swing it. Lake's cousin got a spare room month-to-month."

Mama flinches at Lake's name. "Strangers."

"Honest ones," Eden says.

Lake looks like he wants to disappear and also wants to build a wall around her right there in the living room. "I'll keep her safe," he says.

Mama's mouth says what her face already did: "That was my job."

"Then do it better now," Eden says, not cruel, just final.

She zips the backpack. She looks at me. I am a dam and a river at the same time. "You got oranges," she asks.

I hand her a bag from the counter. "Ugly ones."

"Strongest kind," she says, smiling that old small smile. Then she walks out with Lake.

When the door closes, the house lets out a noise like it was holding its breath too. Mama sits, then stands, then sits again. Caleb goes to the lamp, unscrews the bulb, screws it back, as if that will fix the porch light that popped like a curse. I pick up the papers, stack them, put the rubber bands around the box even though I know they'll snap again tomorrow.

Mama says, to no one, to me, to God maybe, "I wanted a new beginning. I named her for it."

I say, "You got one. You just didn't read the terms."

She looks at me like I'm a judge and she's finally ready to plead. "What do I do."

"Wait," I say. "And when she calls, don't talk about you. Answer what she asks. Don't add poetry."

"Poetry is how I've been breathing," she says.

"Then try prose," I say. "Simple. True."

Night comes in the windows like it always does. Outside, the block is the same size, but I swear the house moved six inches to the left. I clean the kitchen because my hands need to do a job my mouth can't. In the sink a plate has a crack I never saw. I run my thumb along it and think: that's us. Still holding shape. Hairline ready to spread.

I check my phone. A text from Eden: **I'm okay. Don't come.** Then another: **Two squeezes.**

I send back: **Two squeezes. Always.**

I turn off the light and stand in the dark of my mother's kitchen, listening to the old fridge hum like a tired choir. Tomorrow I'll go to work. Mama will make tea. Caleb will drive and pretend the miles mean progress. Somewhere, a man named Leon will feel a wind and not know it's us.

Tomorrow we still won't be done.

But tonight the house learns how to hold a new silence. Not the kind packed with lies. The kind that waits for a true word and refuses to settle for less.

Chapter 19 – The Funeral

He dies on a Tuesday, which feels rude. Dispatch says "cardiac event" at a Pilot off Route 67. A fellow driver finds him sitting in the cab, eyes open like he was still trying to back into the slot. The officer on the phone tells me he looked "peaceful," like that's a feature you can add for a fee.

I'm the one who answers when the county number pops up. I'm the one who calls Ruth. She says "no" three times like she can rewind, then sits down on the kitchen floor with the phone still in her hand as if the floor might have instructions. Eden is at work. I drive over before calling her, because you don't say "he's gone" over speaker while someone is stocking gauze.

We do a small service because the money is small and the circle is smaller. A chapel attached to a funeral home where the carpet is the color of old cherries and the air smells like carnations and chemicals. A woman at the desk says "package B" and I nod because grief apparently comes with options.

The program has a typo—**Calab** instead of **Caleb** on the inside page. I catch it, circle it with my nail, then let it go. I don't have it in me to care about vowels. The photo we pick is one where he's wearing his blue work jacket and looking past the camera like the person he loved was behind the lens. It makes the room softer. Not easier, just softer.

People come because it's the thing you do in this town. Cousins in suits that shine too much. Aunties with tissues up their sleeves. Men from the yard who speak in short sentences: "Good man." "Solid." "Never shorted me." The pastor from Mama's old church offers to say a few words; Mama declines with a smile that doesn't reach any muscle you can name.

We ask for "quiet reflections." Folks interpret that as stories told too loud.

Eden arrives in a plain black dress that looks like it was sewn out of night. She moves like a knife someone wrapped in cloth. Lake stays half a step behind her, shoulders squared the way men square theirs when they can't fix anything but can at least look like a wall.

The chapel has a cross at the front, sure, but it's decorative, not demanding. People sit with the caution of cats in a bathtub. A slideshow plays on a loop. Somebody uses the wrong baby photo once—my cousin Isaiah as a toddler pops up smiling with a popsicle, and half the row snorts before the picture flips. Eden laughs, one breath, then covers her mouth. Grief is rude like that.

We don't have a choir; we have a Bluetooth speaker that drops the connection twice. When "His Eye Is on the Sparrow" finally plays, it sounds like it's coming from someone's trunk. Mama hums under her breath. I do not sing. I do the job of the eldest daughter: hand tissues, receive casseroles, take names.

When it's time for remarks, there's a pause that stretches too long. The funeral director looks at me like I'm the designated talker. I stand because the room says stand.

"My father—" I start, and the first syllable betrays me. It comes out like a door hinge. I clear my throat. "Caleb was a clock. Not perfect. Not always on time. But steady in the way you can set your life by. He loved engines because they made sense, and he loved us even when we didn't. He taught me to check the oil and to keep a granola bar in the glove box and to drive in storms with both hands, no heroics."

People nod like I'm reading instructions out loud. I keep going because stopping would be worse. "We had a loud house. He didn't always know what to say, so he said it with rides to work and cash folded into palms, and a piano he played like truth you can't fit into words. If you ever took a road and felt safer because some man you loved had already driven it, that was him."

I look at the photo, at the jacket, at the ghost of a smile. "We didn't say all our things. Now we won't. That's gonna be a stone I carry. But here's what I know: he showed up for the hard day."

I step down. The room exhales. A man from the yard says something about torque wrenches. Aunt G tells a funny story about how Caleb used to cut all the sandwiches exactly in half at picnics and get mad when kids didn't honor the geometry. We laugh. The laughter does that thing where it falls off the edge and becomes tears again.

Mama does not speak. She sits in the front row with her hands flat on her knees, eyes red, breathing measured like she's afraid if she does it wrong the room will fold. Uncle Theo comes late, hat in hand like remorse is a uniform you can buy. He hugs Mama. She lets him. He tries to catch my eye; I let him catch my shoulder instead. "I'm sorry," he says, and for once he leaves it there.

At the visitation table by the door, a guestbook waits with a pen that dribbles. Eden writes **E. A.** and then, after a second, *Press harder,* she adds —**Daughter.** Seeing it in ink cracks, something in me I didn't know was still intact. She looks up; I look down. We are not going to have a moment here. Not with bad coffee in styrofoam cups and cookies that taste like sugar and dust.

The service ends. It ends the way a cheap song ends—no crescendo, just a button that makes it stop. We file past the closed casket because open wasn't an option with the travel and the time and the money. People touch the wood like it's a door they might still knock on. Mama places her hand there and whispers something to it. She moves her lips like prayer, but I think it's inventory: all the words she held and all the ones she shouldn't have.

Outside, the parking lot heat makes everybody bicker. Cars beep. Kids run where they shouldn't. A cousin waves a flask by the dumpster and gets told off by three women at once. Lake keeps a hand near Eden's elbow, not controlling, just ready. I watch him like I'm grading him. He passes.

We caravan to the cemetery. Someone honks in the procession because they don't know the rules or don't care. Windshields reflect a sky that can't decide between blue and gray. The hill where they set out the green carpet looks like a stage. A man in a suit too big for him reads the psalm about walking through valleys. He reads it too fast. Maybe because he's young, maybe because the wind keeps trying to take the paper.

We lower the box slowly. The straps squeal. People say their last things that won't be last. Little shovels of earth sound like a soft drum. When it's over, folks peel off toward their lives like magnets pulled by larger metal. I stay. Mama stays. Eden stays. Lake hovers with the good sense to hover far enough away.

Mama fingers the edge of the temporary marker. "I should have tried to make him stay," she says. It's to the ground, to the sky, to herself.

"You did," I tell her.

She shakes her head. "Not like this. Not honest."

Eden kneels and presses her palm to the green turf. The gesture looks like a benediction and a dare. "Hi," she says to the air. "It's me. The one you loved the best way you could." Her voice doesn't break. Mine does.

We don't do a group hug. We don't bless the day. We stand in a triangle around a new hole in the earth, and we let the sun hit our necks, and we breathe. That's the best we've ever done together.

Back at the house later, the casseroles are already cooling into new shapes, and the talk is already shifting toward logistics, and I am already starting the long slow job of writing the list of who gets thanked and who gets returned dishes. Eden leans on the counter and peels an orange with a pocketknife like she learned in a movie. She passes me a slice without looking. I eat it. It is the ugliest, sweetest one.

The doorbell rings. Lake opens it. A courier stands there with a manila envelope and a clipboard. "Ruth Afolayan?" he asks.

"I'm Ruth," Mama says.

"Signature," he says. She signs. He leaves. The envelope sits on the table like a dare until Eden slides it over, breaks the seal, and pulls out a single sheet and a small plastic ID card. *Death certificate. DMV temporary.* The state says my father is officially past tense.

On the line marked *Informant,* the name is mine. It looks wrong and true at the same time.

Eden takes a breath, slow. "Tomorrow," she says quietly, "I'm going to look for him."

"The other him," Mama says, voice flat.

"Leon Barker," Eden says. "I'm not promising anything. I'm promising a search."

Mama nods like someone told her the weather and all she can do is grab an umbrella. "Okay."

"I'm not asking your permission."

"I didn't offer it," Mama says, and for once that's not a fight, it's a recognition.

We load plates. We scrape pans. We set out foil. The house hums a tired hum. When the porch light clicks on at dusk, I swear it's brighter than it used to be, like someone finally changed the bulb out for a better kind.

Chapter 20 – The Graveside Talk

A week later, after the family has thinned and the casseroles have evolved into science projects, Eden texts me: **Meet at the hill?** No punctuation. We don't need any.

The cemetery is quiet in the way parking garages are quiet—sound exists, it just lives under things. Grass buzzes with summer. The temporary marker still has the wrong middle initial; I make a note in my head to fix it and then laugh because my head is a junk drawer full of notes I never throw away.

Eden is already there, kneeling again. A grocery bag sits beside her— flowers that don't match, a bottle of water, a small cheap brush. She's cleaning the green dust off the metal plate like it disrespected us on purpose.

"Hey," I say.

"Hey," she says, not looking up. "I brought supplies. I'm domestic now."

"You look the part," I say. Her hair is tied up in a scarf that used to be Mama's. It looks like an inheritance that finally fits.

She finishes the plate, then sits back on her heels. "Lake offered to come," she says. "I told him this one was sisters."

"Thanks," I say, and mean it.

We sit on the edge of the green cloth and look at the dirt like it might look back. For a while we say nothing. That's not unusual; it's our cleanest language.

Finally, Eden says, "I went by the parts place."

"When?"

"Yesterday. In Memphis. Don't cuss. I told you I'd go."

"I can cuss and still be proud," I say.

She smiles a little. "I didn't find him. Company moved. An old guy said they closed that branch two years ago. He called someone, gave me a number for a Lionel, which I pretended was close enough to Leon if men are allowed to rename themselves. The number was dead."

"You okay?"

She thinks about it. "I'm not dead."

"Standard is low."

"Standard is honest." She picks at a string on the cloth. "I'm not on a crusade. I don't need a scene where he cries and we hug and then immediately fight about boundaries. I just want to know if his blood still walks around in somebody else. I want to see the shape of his mouth and say, that's where mine came from. That's all. That's not everything."

"That's a lot," I say.

She nods. "It is."

Wind moves through the oaks like a rumor. Somewhere a car starts and stops. We breathe.

"I keep thinking," she says, "about how Daddy died on the road. That's correct for him. He always loved a lane. But I hate that he died without hearing me say I wasn't leaving. That I just needed distance with honesty inside it."

"He heard you," I say. "Men like him always had a radio on in their head. It's tuned to our house."

She snorts. "You and your metaphors."

"I went prose for a while. I got bored."

We sit with it. Then she says, "I'm mad at Ruth. I'm mad at me for needing her. I'm mad at the whole idea that bodies decide your life and then die on you before you finish the argument."

"Try being mad and making tea," I say. "It's the only combination that doesn't burn something down."

She leans her shoulder into mine. "You're the tea. I'm the match."

"I know," I say. "That's why we didn't burn the house."

We stay like that awhile. Two women with a long list of receipts between them and a fresh grave in front of them. The sun keeps doing its job. Eventually Eden reaches into the bag and pulls out a small spiral notebook and a pen. She writes something, tears the page out carefully, folds it, and presses it under the edge of the marker where the grass will hold it.

"You want to tell me what that was," I ask.

"No," she says. "But I'll tell you this: it wasn't forgiveness. Not yet. It was a receipt."

"Proof of purchase?"

"Proof of cost," she says. "Proof I paid."

We stand. She dusts off her knees. "Okay," she says, the way she said it on Ama's porch. It still doesn't mean okay; it means next.

"Next is what," I ask.

"I go back to work. I stop jumping when the mail comes. I maybe try to find a Lionel who used to be a Leon and ask him one question with no drama words. I let Ruth call me and I don't answer if I'm not ready. I buy oranges that look like they fell out of a tree and rolled through a fight. I learn how to sleep without the maps on the wall. I let Lake hang a picture and hate where he puts it and say so without starting a war. I tell the truth when it costs."

"That's a list," I say. "Now you sound like me."

"I'm stealing your brand," she says.

We start walking back to the car. Halfway there, we stop. It's the spot where the hill flattens and you can see the row of stones that all look like brothers. Eden turns to me. "Thank you," she says.

"For what."

"For not playing stenographer when I needed a sister," she says. "For saying the ugly sentences. For holding the oranges."

I nod. I don't cry because I already paid for that today.

At the car, she squeezes my hand twice. I squeeze back twice. The code still works. We get in. The engine turns over. The radio comes on mid-song, some old R&B track about love being a house you can't afford. We laugh, not because it's funny but because it's accurate.

I drive us home the long way, down the streets we've drawn a hundred times, past the liquor store with the flickering E, past Mr. Rivera's cart where the good empanadas live, past the corner where kids chalk hopscotch grids like maps to better days. We don't talk much. We don't need to.

When we pull up to Mama's, the porch light is on. It's brighter than I remember. Inside, I can see through the window that the blue file box is on the table. The rubber bands are lying beside it, snapped and useless. The lid is open. There's a single sheet of paper on top.

Eden looks at me. I look at her. We go in.

Ruth is at the sink, washing the same cup over and over like it holds the riddle. She turns when the door opens. For a second her face is the face of an ordinary woman in an ordinary kitchen with two daughters at the door. Then it's her face again: scared, stubborn, softer than she wants to be.

"I left you something," she says to Eden, voice steady for the first time in a long time.

On the paper is Eden's birth certificate. Not the altered copy with fresh ink. The original, creased from years of hiding. In the box corner, another paper, folded small: a one-line address, half a phone number, the name **BARKER** written in Mama's hand next to a date that's only two weeks old.

"I looked again," Ruth says. "I shouldn't have kept it. I did. I don't want to anymore."

Eden doesn't reach for it. Not yet. She looks at Ruth long enough that the room gets real quiet. "Okay," she says. "Thank you."

There's no hug. There's no cinematic soundtrack swell. There's a kettle on the stove that chooses this moment to click and hum its way to a boil. Ruth turns the flame off and looks at me. I nod toward the cabinet where the good mugs are. She takes them down. No one says "forgiveness." No one says "start over." We say "do you want lemon" and "no, just plain" and "sugar's on the left."

We sit with our identical cups at the table where we've lied and laughed and counted bills. Eden finally reaches for the paper and slides it into her bag, slow, like it's heavy. She looks at both of us and she looks like all the women we came from and none of them, too.

"Two squeezes," she says softly, and under the table she finds my hand and Ruth's and squeezes each of us twice, separate, equal, no promises beyond this room but no more pretending either.

It's not a miracle. It's not a curse lifted. It's the thing we get: a small good moment in a kitchen that's held worse.

Later, when I walk back to my apartment, the night feels like it's not trying to sell me something. I climb the creaky stairs, open the door, and stand in the dark a second because I like the way the city breathes when it thinks you're not listening. I pull the box of notebooks down from my shelf—the ones with my receipts and my questions and my attempts at keeping a wild life filed.

take the first one—the one that starts **Bracelet says 3:12**—and I sit on the floor and tear out a page. Then another. Then another. Not to burn. Not to erase. To let go of the idea that I'm the librarian for everyone's sins.

I save a few pages because I am still me. I slide the rest into a grocery bag. Tomorrow the recycling truck will take them away and bleach them into new pulp and someone will print grocery coupons on them and some tired woman will save a dollar and it will mean more than poetry.

Before bed, I text Eden: **You good?**

She texts back: **No. But I'm honest.**

I smile. I set my phone down. I leave the window cracked. Somewhere a siren starts and then stops, like even trouble needs to rest.

Morning will come. We'll make tea. We'll answer only what's asked. We'll buy ugly oranges and eat them over the sink so the juice doesn't stain. We'll call what happened what it is and let the labels sit without decorating them. We'll learn, slowly, the shape of a house where truth lives with us and doesn't need to be hidden in a blue box.

We won't be fixed. We'll be true. That's better. That's enough.

The End.

About the Author

Elfreeda Starr Miles is an accomplished CPA and lawyer. She has been writing for years but has finally decided that now is the time to publish and let others enjoy her dramatic and witty stories, many based on true events.

She is the mother of two. She enjoys horticulture, gardening, and is a fantastic cook.

Look for other titles that will wow you, entertain you and move you.